First Facts®

EXTREME PLANET

THE HOTTEST PLACES ON EARTH

by Jennifer M. Besel

Consultant:
Randall S. Cerveny, PhD
President's Professor, School of Geographical Sciences
Arizona State University, Tempe

CAPSTONE PRESS
a capstone imprint

First Facts is published by Capstone Press,
151 Good Counsel Drive, P.O. Box 669, Mankato, Minnesota 56002.
www.capstonepress.com

092009
005618CGS10

 Books published by Capstone Press are manufactured with paper
containing at least 10 percent post-consumer waste.

Library of Congress Cataloging-in-Publication Data
Besel, Jennifer M.
  The hottest places on Earth / by Jennifer M. Besel.
    p. cm. — (First facts. Extreme planet)
    Summary: "An introduction to the hottest places on Earth, including maps and colorful
photographs" — Provided by publisher.
    Includes bibliographical references and index.
    ISBN 978-1-4296-3964-4 (library binding)
    1. Climatic extremes — Juvenile literature. 2. Tropics — Description and travel — Juvenile literature.
3. Death Valley (Calif. and Nev.) — Juvenile literature. 4. Hydrothermal vents — Juvenile literature. 5.
Earth — Mantle — Juvenile literature. I. Title. II. Series.
QC981.8.C53B475 2010
910.913 — dc22   2009026039

Editorial credits
Erika L. Shores, editor; Ted Williams, designer, Svetlana Zhurkin, media researcher;
  Eric Manske, production specialist

Photo credits
Alamy/Eric Chahi, 15; Ian Leonard, 13; Linda Weissenberger, 10
Corbis/Ralph White, 19
iStockphoto/Goldmund Photography, cover, 7
Photodisc, 21
Shutterstock/Galyna Andrushko, 5
University of Washington, School of Oceanography, 16
Visuals Unlimited/Dr. Richard Roscoe, 9

Essential content terms are **bold** and are defined at the bottom of the spread where they first appear.

TABLE OF CONTENTS

A RECIPE FOR HEAT

Every day, the sun heats the earth. In some places, that heat reaches extremes. Areas that don't get much rain have the hottest air temperatures. Then add low **elevation** and no wind to the mix. That's a recipe for powerful heat.

High temperatures happen around the world. Some hot spots are even inside the earth! Check out seven of the planet's hottest places.

elevation — the height above sea level

BANGKOK, THAILAND

Bangkok, Thailand, is one hot city. The average daytime temperature there is 90° F (32° C). But people in Bangkok also deal with high **humidity**. The wet, heavy air makes it feel more like a sticky 120° F (49° C.)

> **humidity** — the measure of the moisture in the air

! Temperatures are listed in degrees Fahrenheit or Celsius. In this book, temperatures are shown with the degree symbol (°) and F for Fahrenheit or C for Celsius.

BANGKOK, THAILAND

6 DALLOL, ETHIOPIA

Dallol, Ethiopia, sits in a valley more than 300 feet (91 meters) below **sea level**. The valley acts like a bowl, trapping heat inside. The average monthly temperature in Dallol never drops below 93° F (34° C). Few people live in this area.

sea level — the average level of the ocean's surface; sea level is a starting point from which to measure height or depth.

DALLOL, ETHIOPIA

N W E S

EXTREME FACT!

Water found just below ground in areas of Dallol bubbles up to the surface. The water evaporates and turns the ground different colors.

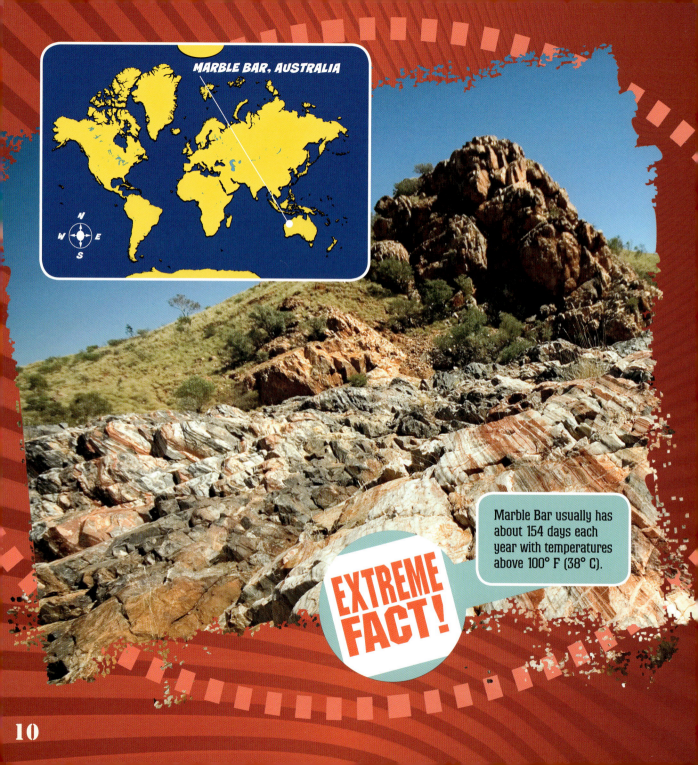

MARBLE BAR, AUSTRALIA

Marble Bar usually has about 154 days each year with temperatures above 100° F (38° C).

EXTREME FACT!

MARBLE BAR, AUSTRALIA

5

A record-setting hot spell made Marble Bar famous. This small town is located in the northwest desert of Australia. On October 31, 1923, temperatures soared above 100° F (38° C). Temperatures stayed that high for 160 straight days.

desert — an area where very little rain falls

11

4 FURNACE CREEK RANCH, CALIFORNIA

Furnace Creek Ranch is located in California's desert area called Death Valley. Summer temperatures in Death Valley average 112° F (44° C).

Furnace Creek Ranch holds the record for hottest temperature in the western **hemisphere**. On October 7, 1913, the temperature hit 134° F (57° C).

hemisphere — one half of the earth

FURNACE CREEK RANCH,
CALIFORNIA

13

3 AL AZIZIYAH, LIBYA

Al Aziziyah is a small town in Africa's Sahara desert. On September 13, 1922, this town made history. The temperature hit 136° F (58° C). This air temperature is the hottest ever recorded on earth.

Al Aziziyah: AHL ah-zee-zee-YAH

Life goes on in this hot spot despite of the temperatures. Al Aziziyah is a major trade center for people who live in the Sahara desert.

EXTREME FACT!

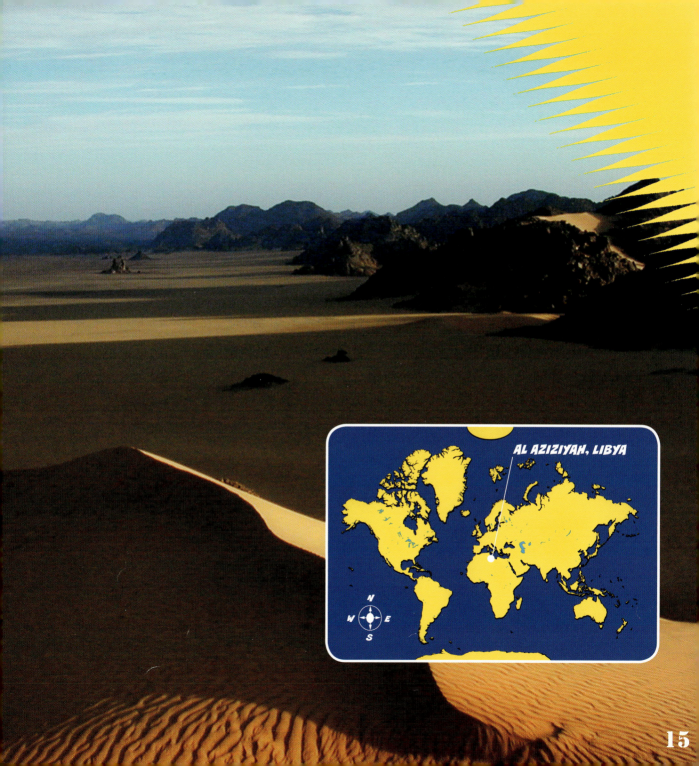

AL AZIZIYAH, LIBYA

15

HYDROTHERMAL VENTS

Deep inside the earth, **molten** rocks produce powerful heat. The rocks above the molten rocks shift around and make cracks.

Beneath the ocean, water seeps into those cracks. The water flows deep into the earth. The molten rocks heat the water. The superhot water bursts back to the surface from a **hydrothermal vent**.

molten — to be in a very hot, nearly liquid state

hydrothermal vent — a crack that allows superheated steam to escape from deep in the earth

Water spewing from a hydrothermal vent reaches 750° F (400° C). That's hot enough to melt lead!

Some creatures live inside these vents. Tubeworms, eyeless shrimp, and huge clams call the burning hot water home.

EXTREME FACT!

Hydrothermal vents on land are called geysers. Old Faithful is a geyser in Yellowstone National Park in Wyoming.

TUBEWORMS

1 The Earth's Core

The hottest place on earth is actually inside the planet. Molten rocks are found as deep as 4,000 miles (6,437 kilometers) below ground in an area near the earth's core. Scientists recorded a temperature of 6,650° F (3,677° C) near the core. The core is definitely the planet's hottest spot!

core — the inner part of earth that is made of metal, rocks, and melted rock

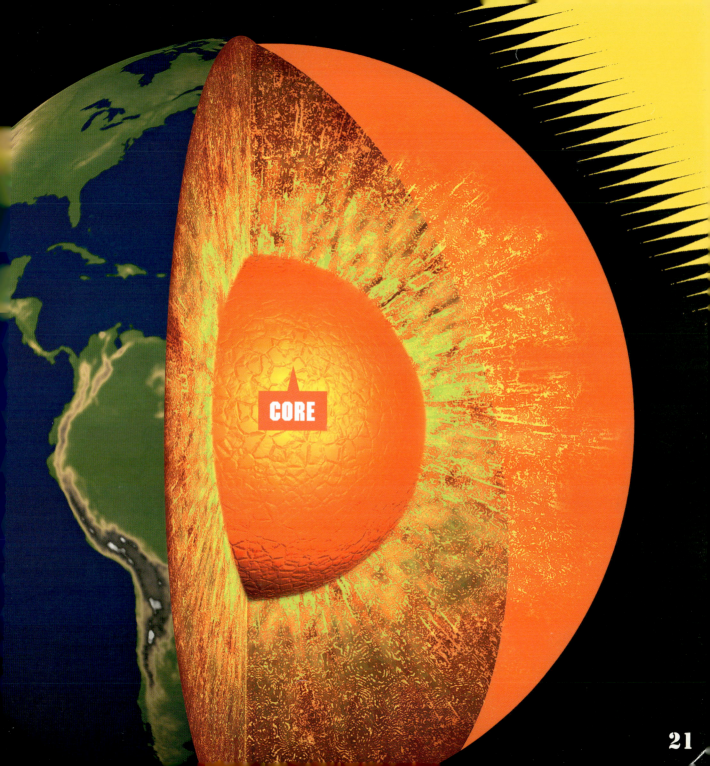

CORE

GLOSSARY

core (KOR) — the inner part of earth that is made of metal, rocks, and melted rock

desert (DEZ-urt) — an area where very little rain falls

elevation (el-uh-VAY-shuhn) — the height above sea level; sea level is defined as zero elevation.

hemisphere (HEM-uhss-fihr) — one half of the earth

humidity (hyoo-MIH-du-tee) — the measure of the moisture in the air

hydrothermal vent (hi-dro-THUR-muhl VENT) — a hot water spring or geyser erupting on the ocean floor or on land

molten (MOLE-tuhn) — to be in a very hot, nearly liquid state

sea level (SEE LEV-uhl) — the average level of the ocean's surface; sea level is a starting point from which to measure height or depth.

READ MORE

Bauman, Amy. *Earth's Crust and Core.* Planet Earth. Pleasantville, N.Y.: Gareth Stevens, 2008.

Hirschmann, Kris, and Ryan Herndon, ed. *Guinness World Records, Up Close: Wild Weather.* New York: Scholastic, 2007.

Jackson, Kay. *Explore the Desert.* Explore the Biomes. Mankato, Minn.: Capstone Press, 2007.

INTERNET SITES

FactHound offers a safe, fun way to find Internet sites related to this book. All of the sites on FactHound have been researched by our staff.

Here's all you do:

Visit *www.facthound.com*

FactHound will fetch the best sites for you!

INDEX